★ GREAT SPORTS TEAMS ★

THE PITTSBURGH

STEELERS

FOOTBALL TEAM

William W. Lace

Enslow Publishers, Inc.

44 Fadem Road   PO Box 38
Box 699   Aldershot
Springfield, NJ 07081 Hants GU12 6BP
USA   UK

Library of Congress Cataloging-in-Publication Data

Lace, William W.
    The Pittsburgh Steelers football team / William W. Lace.
        p. cm. — (Great sports teams)
    Includes bibliographical references (p. 43) and index.
    Summary: Covers the history of the team that has played in Pittsburgh for more that sixty years, discussing some key players, coaches, and important games.
    ISBN 0-7660-1099-6
    1. Pittsburgh Steelers (Football team)—History—Juvenile literature.
    [1. Pittsburgh Steelers (Football team)—History. 2. Football—History.]
    I. Title. II. Series.
    GV956.P57L33   1999
    796.332'64'0974886—dc21   98-9664
                                                              CIP
                                                               AC

Printed in the United States of America

10 9 8 7 6 5 4 3 2 1

Illustration Credits: AP/Wide World Photos

Cover Illustration: AP/Wide World Photos

Cover Description: Jerome Bettis, running back

CONTENTS

*A*s his protection starts to break down, Terry Bradshaw is flushed out of the pocket.

IMMACULATE RECEPTION

The Pittsburgh Steelers' 1972 dream season was about to become a nightmare. They had won the Central Division of the National Football League's American Conference with an 11–3 record. It was the first championship of any kind in the Steelers' forty-year history. Now, before more than fifty thousand fans in Pittsburgh's Three Rivers Stadium, the Steelers were trying for another first—their first-ever postseason victory.

The Steelers trailed the Oakland Raiders, 7–6. They had the ball on their own 40-yard line, but it was fourth down, and only twenty-two seconds remained in the game. In the press box, team owner Art Rooney, Sr., boarded the elevator, heading for the dressing room. It looked like another case of what Pittsburgh fans always called SOS—Same Old Steelers.

In the huddle, quarterback Terry Bradshaw called the play—"Sixty-six pass." He hoped to pick up about thirty yards, enough to give kicker Roy Gerela a chance at a winning field goal. The team trotted to the line of scrimmage.

"The Greatest Pass"

Bradshaw, who had played poorly up to that point, suddenly "was faced with throwing the greatest pass of my life."[1] He barked out the signals, took the snap from the center, and faded back, looking for primary receiver Barry Pearson. Pearson was covered. The Raiders defensive linemen were getting closer, clutching at his jersey.

Meanwhile, running back Franco Harris, who was supposed to be blocking for Bradshaw, had drifted out of the backfield. "I had just sensed that Terry was scrambling for his life," Harris said, "so I thought I'd go downfield. I'd give him another receiver."[2] Harris was wide open. Frantically, he waved at Bradshaw. Bradshaw did not see him.

Bradshaw ducked away from the Oakland rush. He looked for his No. 2 receiver, John "Frenchy" Fuqua, who was running about thirty yards downfield. Just before Bradshaw was decked by the Raiders, he fired the ball toward Fuqua.

Midair Collision

The pass was right on target. But as Fuqua leaped to catch it, Oakland defensive back Jack Tatum was there, too. The ball, Fuqua, and Tatum met in midair. Fuqua crashed to the ground. The ball sailed back

The Pittsburgh Steelers Football Team

toward the line of scrimmage. The Pittsburgh crowd groaned.

Then, seemingly out of nowhere, came Harris. On a dead run, he caught the ball just inches off the ground and sprinted for the Oakland goal line. The Raiders, stunned, were slow to react. Only Jimmy Warren had a chance to catch Harris. Harris brushed off Warren with a stiff-arm and raced into the end zone.

The officials hesitated and looked at each other. Was it a touchdown? According to the rules at that time, if the ball had been batted from Fuqua to Harris,

After grabbing Bradshaw's deflected pass, Franco Harris ran for the end zone. Escaping Raiders defensive back Jimmy Warren, Harris scored the game-winning touchdown.

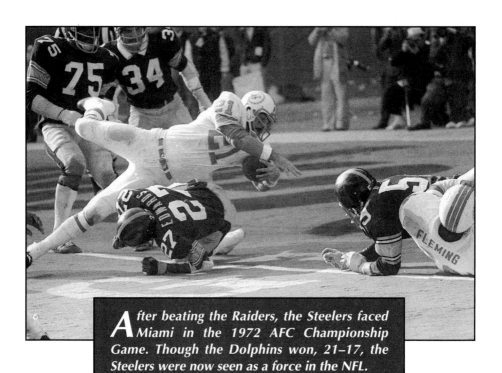

After beating the Raiders, the Steelers faced Miami in the 1972 AFC Championship Game. Though the Dolphins won, 21–17, the Steelers were now seen as a force in the NFL.

it was an incomplete pass. If Tatum had swatted it to Harris, the play counted. Referee Fred Swearingen used a field telephone to confer with league official Art McNally, who was in the press box. Finally, he signaled a touchdown. The crowd roared.

Rooney Gets the News

At that moment, Art Rooney, Sr., emerged from the elevator. A security guard grabbed his hand and shook it. "You won! You won!" he shouted.[3] Rooney had missed the "Immaculate Reception," the most famous play in NFL history.

"Luck?" said Bradshaw after the game. "Sure, we were lucky. After forty years, why shouldn't Pittsburgh get lucky? Who deserves it more?"[4]

The next week, Pittsburgh played the Miami Dolphins for the AFC Championship and a spot in the Super Bowl. Once more, trailing with only seconds left, the Steelers got the ball. Would there be another miracle? Not this time. A Bradshaw pass was intercepted by Terry Kolen, and the Dolphins won, 21–17. The Steelers' season was over, but they had shown everyone they were no longer the "Same Old Steelers." They were on the edge of becoming one of the NFL's greatest teams ever.

*S*teelers quarterback/running back Byron "Whizzer" White, won the 1938 rushing title. White played football to help pay for law school and later became a Supreme Court justice.

THE LONG CLIMB

n 1933, Pittsburgh sports promoter Art Rooney, Sr., bought an NFL franchise for two thousand five hundred dollars. He already had a team, the semipro Majestic Radios. He renamed it the Pittsburgh Pirates, like the baseball team.

At the end of the 1940 season, Rooney sold the team to Alexis Thompson, who officially moved it to Philadelphia. Meanwhile, Rooney bought a share of the Philadelphia Eagles and, with co-owner Bert Bell, moved that team to Pittsburgh.

Rooney thought the new team deserved a new name. A contest was held, and the name Steelers was selected in the spring of 1941. The team would continue to be known as the Steelers except for two years during World War II. It was called the Steagles when it was combined with the Philadelphia Eagles in 1943 and the Carpets when it was combined with the Chicago Cardinals in 1944.

After Rooney's team lost its first game, 23–2, to the New York Giants, he said, "The fans did not get their money's worth today."[1] The fans did not often get their money's worth in those early years. It would be 1942 before the team had a winning season.

Great Players, No Titles

Horses were Rooney's main interest. His football team was more of a hobby. Coaches came and went. There were a few great players such as Johnny Blood, Byron "Whizzer" White (who played one season for the Steelers and ultimately became a justice on the United States Supreme Court), and "Bullet Bill" Dudley, but not enough to produce a championship.

By 1945, the Steelers had had only two winning seasons. Only fifteen hundred season tickets were sold that year. Rooney decided to get serious about the team. He hired Dr. John "Jock" Sutherland, who had been a successful coach in both college and pro football.

Season ticket sales in 1946 soared to twenty-two thousand because of Sutherland's popularity with Pittsburgh fans. The Steelers improved, too. In 1947, they went 8–4 and tied for the Eastern Conference championship but lost the playoff, 21–0, to the Philadelphia Eagles. "If it hadn't been for Jock," Rooney said years later, "someone other than myself would own the Steelers today."[2]

Starting Over

The good times did not last. After Sutherland died of a brain tumor in 1948, the Steelers began to go

The Pittsburgh Steelers Football Team

*B*uddy Parker is shown here with (l to r) quarterbacks Earl Morrell, Len Dawson, Jack Kemp, and fullback Fran Rogel.

downhill. The next nine years produced only one winning season. Once more, Rooney knew something had to be done. He hired Buddy Parker, who had coached Detroit to two NFL championships.

Parker believed in building a team with veteran players rather than rookies. During his eight years as coach, the Steelers traded most of their high choices in the college draft for veterans such as quarterback Bobby Layne, defensive tackle Gene "Big Daddy" Lipscomb, and fullback John Henry Johnson.

The Long Climb

Parker's tactics brought results. The Steelers enjoyed back-to-back winning seasons in 1958 and 1959. In 1962, they went 9–5, finishing second in the Eastern Conference.

Still, the team failed to win a championship. It was also hurt by questionable front-office decisions. In 1955, the Steelers made one of football's greatest mistakes, cutting rookie Johnny Unitas, a future Hall of Fame quarterback. In 1957, Parker cut two more rookie quarterbacks, Len Dawson and Jack Kemp. Both would win professional titles elsewhere. Finally, when one of his trades was blocked in 1965 by Steelers Vice-President Dan Rooney, the owner's son, Parker quit as coach.

Another Change

Over the next four seasons, the Steelers went from bad to worse. After a 2–11–1 season in 1968, it was time for another coaching change. The Rooneys settled on a young Baltimore Colts assistant named Chuck Noll. "The more I talked with him, [the more I knew] Noll was the guy," Dan Rooney said. "We finally did it right."[3]

Unlike Parker, Noll built his teams through the draft. In the next few years, such players as "Mean" Joe Greene, Terry Bradshaw, Mel Blount, Lynn Swann, and Franco Harris arrived. These and others would bring Pittsburgh four Super Bowl titles and make them the Team of the Seventies.

Eventually, however, the stars of the 1970s faded. After a 7–9 record in 1991—only his seventh losing

The Pittsburgh Steelers Football Team

Running past Cleveland fullback Tommy Vardell, Rod Woodson tries to score on his interception return. Woodson was selected to the AFC All-Pro Team seven times as a Steeler.

season in twenty-three years—Noll gave way to Bill Cowher.

It was time for a new generation of stars—Barry Foster, Kordell Stewart, Rod Woodson—who would soon have the Steelers winning division championships and back in the Super Bowl.

*L*ooking downfield, Steelers quarterback Bobby Layne loads up for a bomb. Known as a fierce competitor, Layne was also an excellent leader.

MEN OF STEEL

Some of the most talented and colorful players in football history have worn Pittsburgh's black and gold. Some have been elected to the Pro Football Hall of Fame, and many more will be remembered as long as there are Steelers' fans.

Bobby Layne

In 1958, the Steelers wanted a quarterback and a leader. By trading for Bobby Layne, they got both. "When he went on the field, Bobby Layne was in charge," said Art Rooney, Sr.[1]

In his very first game for the Steelers, facing third down and short, he told his teammates, "We don't have to squeeze out a foot and a half when we can score a touchdown."[2] Instead of a running play, he threw deep for a touchdown, and the Steelers went on to win, 24–3.

Layne was not especially big. He did not have a great arm. He did, however, have a fierce desire to win. "I don't care if we're just playing showdown [poker] for a nickel a hand," he once said. "I want to beat your brains in."[3]

Layne was elected to the Hall of Fame in 1967.

Joe Greene

Some fans had their doubts when the Steelers made Joe Greene their top draft choice in 1969, but Chuck Noll was not worried. "I had never seen anybody block him one-on-one," Noll said. "With his great quickness, speed, and strength, he has pretty much everything you're looking for."[4]

Greene was the anchor of the famous "Steel Curtain" defense that helped the Steelers win four Super Bowls. A relentless pass rusher, he unofficially recorded 66 quarterback sacks in his thirteen seasons. He was a Pro Bowl selection ten times and was elected to the Hall of Fame in 1987.

Greene was a perfect blend of size and speed. "If you let him, he can blow right by you before you react," said New England Patriots lineman Len St. Jean.[5]

Terry Bradshaw

With only about three minutes left in Super Bowl IX, Terry Bradshaw took the snap, rolled right, and fired a touchdown pass to Larry Brown. That pass clinched the Steelers' first-ever Super Bowl championship.

The Pittsburgh Steelers Football Team

*F*ollowing the action, Franco Harris is about to jump into the play. Harris holds the Super Bowl record for most career rushing yards.

"A feeling of peace came over me," Bradshaw later wrote, "and made me feel like saying, 'Hey, I belong out here.'"[6]

Bradshaw had not always had confidence in himself. He was the Steelers' top draft pick in 1970 but started out playing poorly, and he was eventually benched by Coach Chuck Noll. He finally took over at quarterback for good midway through the 1972 season, and eventually he was named Most Valuable Player in Super Bowls XIII and XIV. He retired in 1983 as the team's all-time passing leader and was named to the Hall of Fame in 1989.

Franco Harris

After the 1972 draft, Steelers coach Chuck Noll said, "We were looking for someone with size, speed, and catching ability. Franco was our man."[7] Four games into the season, however, Noll might have had other thoughts. His top draft pick had gained only 79 yards.

Noll decided to give Harris one more chance, starting him against Houston. "I told myself just to go at them. Go straight and hard," Harris said.[8] He gained 115 yards against the Oilers and went on to be named NFL Rookie of the Year.

Harris gained 12,120 yards in his career—third-best in NFL history at the time of his retirement. He was inducted into the Hall of Fame in 1990.

Greg Lloyd

Greg Lloyd, only the thirtieth linebacker chosen in the 1987 draft, became one of the very best in the NFL. He was the heart of the Steelers defense that went to Super Bowl XXX.

Going into the 1998 season, Lloyd had more career quarterback sacks—53.5—than any other Steelers linebacker. He had played in five Pro Bowls and has been a consensus all-pro twice.

Lloyd is a fierce competitor who's not afraid to risk injury. "We want to play the game in an aggressive and physical nature, and he's a big part of our success," said Pittsburgh director of football operations Tom Donahoe. "Leadership, intensity—Greg brings them to work every day."[9]

Jerome Bettis

In 1996, hoping to boost their ground game, the Steelers signed Jerome Bettis. The former Notre Dame

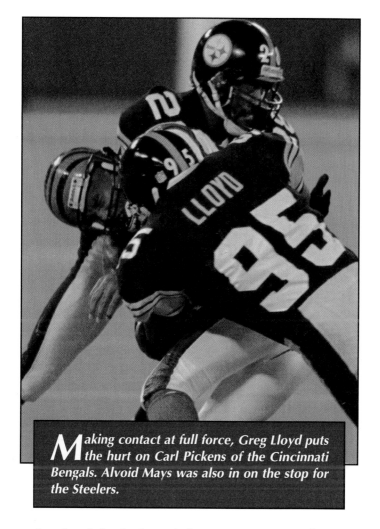

Making contact at full force, Greg Lloyd puts the hurt on Carl Pickens of the Cincinnati Bengals. Alvoid Mays was also in on the stop for the Steelers.

running back had played three seasons for the Rams, rushing for more than 1,000 yards in both 1993 and 1994.

Bettis responded to the move by gaining 1,431 yards, third behind Barry Sanders of Detroit and Terrell Davis of Denver. "This guy has been a big part of it [the Steelers offense]," said Coach Bill Cowher, "and he'll be a big part of it again."[10]

Art Rooney, Sr., was one of the most popular owners in sports. He is shown here with three of the four Lombardi trophies that the Steelers were awarded as Super Bowl champs.

FROM CHIEF TO COWHER

From 1933 until his death in 1988, Art Rooney, Sr., was the guiding light for the Pittsburgh Steelers. Although he was known affectionately as the Chief, Rooney allowed his coaches to run the team. Buddy Parker and Chuck Noll produced winners, and Bill Cowher continued that tradition.

Art Rooney, Sr.

After the Steelers' first-ever Super Bowl victory, the jubilant players shouted, "Chief! Chief! Chief!" Then, they presented Art Rooney, Sr., with the game ball.

The Pittsburgh owner was afraid he might cry. "I was afraid that would happen to me on national television," he said. "I didn't want to be embarrassed."[1]

Rooney always seemed to care more for his players than other owners did, and it paid off. "That was the edge we had as a football team," said Joe Greene.

"The Cowboys, the Raiders, all of those people were equal to us in terms of talent. We did it for the Chief."[2]

Rooney had a special relationship with his coaches, too. Later, he said that if he had taken a more active role from the beginning, he "would have been a help. I don't think we would have had so many bad years."[3]

When Rooney died, the leadership of the team stayed in the family. His sons had been helping him run the team for years. Everyone knew, however, that there would never be another Chief. "I knew only one legend in my entire life," wrote Terry Bradshaw, "and that was Art Rooney."[4]

Buddy Parker

When Parker became head coach in 1957, the Steelers had not had a winning season in eight years. So when his team went 6–6, somebody told Parker it was a good start. "Good, hell," snapped Parker. "Since when is five hundred and third place good?"[5]

Parker was a very impatient coach. He wanted to win right now, not at some time in the future. To do so, he traded away draft choices for veteran players.

He was impatient with his teams, too. If a player had a bad game, Parker might abruptly cut him from the team. Parker once was so angry after a loss that he sent a telegram to NFL commissioner Bert Bell, cutting the entire team. When Bell called him, Parker said, "Oh, forget it, Bert. Tear it up. You know me on Sunday night after I lose a ball game."[6]

Chuck Noll will always be remembered as one of the best head coaches in NFL history. In July 1993, Noll was inducted into the Pro Football Hall of Fame.

Although his trades would cost the Steelers in future years, Parker succeeded in winning. His 1962 team went 9–5, good enough for second in the Eastern Division.

Chuck Noll

Noll wanted to win just as badly as Parker. "Forget that respectable stuff," he said after becoming head coach in 1969. "We're aiming for a championship now."[7]

*B*ill Cowher took over as Steelers head coach in 1992 and returned the Steelers to their winning ways. From 1992–97, Cowher's teams won five division titles.

Unlike Parker, however, Noll believed in building through the draft. Even when his first team went 1–13, Noll saw progress. "It's not the kind of thing you'd notice," he said, "but slowly, but surely, we're getting better."[8]

Through solid drafts and patience with his young players, Noll brought the Steelers from the NFL's basement all the way to four championships. He is the first coach ever to win four Super Bowls.

The trick, said Dan Rooney, was giving the players confidence. "He made these guys believe in themselves," Rooney said. "And that's what they needed more than anything."[9]

Bill Cowher

When Bill Cowher took over from Chuck Noll as head coach in 1992, almost all the great Super Bowl veterans—Bradshaw, Greene, Harris, and the rest—had retired. But Cowher was looking to the future, not the past. "Bill's approach from the beginning," said Tom Donahoe, "was that there was a good nucleus here, and there's no reason we can't put something together and start winning some football games."[10]

That's exactly what Cowher did. In fact, his 53 regular-season wins in his first five years was the third-best record in NFL history.

Like Noll before him, Cowher believes that confidence wins games. "If you stay at things," he said, "and don't ever stop believing, you make your own good fortune."[11]

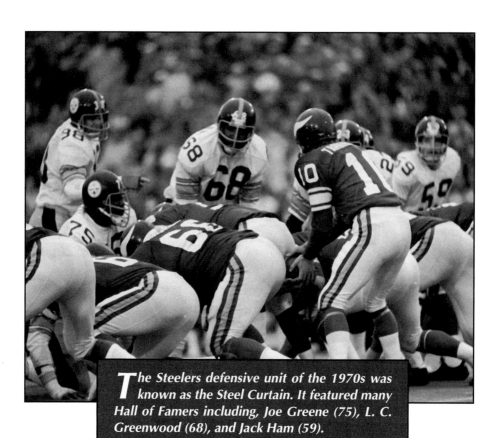

*T*he Steelers defensive unit of the 1970s was known as the Steel Curtain. It featured many Hall of Famers including, Joe Greene (75), L. C. Greenwood (68), and Jack Ham (59).

SUPER TIMES FOUR

Winning is like making Irish stew," Art Rooney, Sr., once wrote. "You must blend the ingredients properly."[1] The Pittsburgh Steelers have had that winning blend only a few times in their long history, but when they were really cooking, they were among the very best.

1974: Breakthrough

In 1971, former Green Bay Packers coach Vince Lombardi said, "I look for the Steelers to be the team of the future. Just remember I said that."[2] Just three years later, Lombardi's prediction had come true.

The 1974 Steelers lineup was dotted with rookies, but what rookies—Lynn Swann, Jack Lambert, John Stallworth, and Mike Webster. These future Pro Bowlers, along with the passing of Terry Bradshaw and the running of Franco Harris, propelled Pittsburgh to a 10–3–1 regular season record.

The Buffalo Bills were the Steelers' first playoff victims, falling 32–14. The Steelers then came from behind to beat Oakland, 24–13, earning a spot in Super Bowl IX. There, the Steel Curtain defense held the Minnesota Vikings to only 119 yards of total offense in a 16–6 victory.

"What emerged was a team," said running back Rocky Bleier, "guys who believed we could do things."[3]

1975: Repeat

"It's like walking on a high wire," said Coach Chuck Noll after his team reached the top in 1974. "You must concentrate on what you're doing. If you look down, you'll fall off."[4] But the Steelers weren't looking down in 1975—only forward.

This was the year the Steel Curtain defense was at its best. Led by the front four of "Mean" Joe Greene, L. C. Greenwood, Ernie Holmes, and Dwight White, the Steelers allowed only 162 points during a 12–2 regular season.

After polishing off Baltimore and Oakland in the playoffs, Pittsburgh faced the Dallas Cowboys in Super Bowl X in Miami, Florida. It was a close, hard-fought game, and with three minutes left, the Steelers—clinging to a 15–10 lead—faced a crucial third down.

Bradshaw called for a long pass, hoping to fool the Cowboys. He escaped the first onrushing defender and then, just as he was hit, launched the ball far downfield. Swann raced past the Dallas secondary, caught the ball at the 5-yard line, and went in for what

The Pittsburgh Steelers Football Team

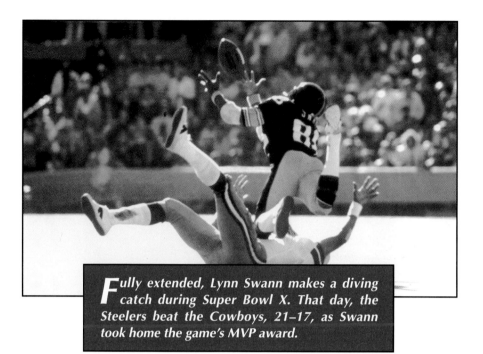

*F*ully extended, Lynn Swann makes a diving catch during Super Bowl X. That day, the Steelers beat the Cowboys, 21–17, as Swann took home the game's MVP award.

proved to be the winning touchdown. It was his fourth catch of the afternoon—for a total of 164 yards. Swann was named Most Valuable Player, and the Steelers had won back-to-back Super Bowls.

1978: Best Ever?

The 1978 Steelers were perhaps the best team in the history of professional football. With Harris rushing for more than a thousand yards for the sixth straight year and Bradshaw leading the AFC in passing yardage with 2,915, Pittsburgh romped through the regular season with a 14–2 record.

It seemed as if the NFL championship would come just as easily. The Steelers first crushed the Denver Broncos, 33–10, and then demolished the Houston

*S*teelers center Mike Webster was one of the many Hall of Fame players that played on the great Steelers teams of the 1970s.

Oilers, 34–5, to earn a return trip to Miami for Super Bowl XIII. There, the easy road ended, and Chuck Noll's troops had the fight of their life against the Cowboys.

The Steelers built a 35–17 lead and appeared to have matters under control, but Roger Staubach and the Cowboys fought back, and the Steelers barely escaped with a 35–31 victory. Experts consider this game to be one of the best Super Bowls ever played. Bradshaw was brilliant, passing for 318 yards and 4 touchdowns.

The Pittsburgh Steelers Football Team

1979: Team of the Decade

In 1979, the Steelers again made the trip to the Super Bowl look easy, coasting to a 12–4 regular-season record and posting easy playoff victories over Miami, 34–13, and Houston, 27–13. Bradshaw was better than ever, throwing for a team-record 3,724 yards.

Everyone expected Pittsburgh to have an easy time in Super Bowl XIV in Los Angeles. The Steelers' opponents, the Los Angeles Rams, had barely made it into the playoffs with a 9–7 regular season record, and then squeaked by Dallas and Tampa Bay to get to the championship game.

The Steelers were a big twelve-point favorite, but the Rams had other ideas. Led by backup quarterback Vince Ferragamo, they led 13–10 at halftime and were still ahead, 19–17, deep in the third quarter.

Moments after the Rams regained the lead, however, Bradshaw lofted the ball deep for John Stallworth, who made an unbelievable catch, bending backward while running full-stride. The play went 74 yards for a touchdown, and the Steelers went on to win, 31–19. "It was crushing to play good defense and have something like that happen," said the Rams' Fred Dryer. "That can break your back."[5]

Seven Steelers of the 1970s—Terry Bradshaw, Mel Blount, Joe Greene, Franco Harris, Jack Ham, Jack Lambert, and Mike Webster—have been elected to the Pro Football Hall of Fame. "There's just something intangible in being part of that group," said tackle Jon Kolb. "Although we'll never be together again, we'll never lose that glow inside."[6]

*T*he Steelers returned to the Super Bowl after the 1995 season. Pittsburgh running back Bam Morris struggles to gain yardage against the Cowboys defense.

1990s AND BEYOND

Super Bowl XIV was the end of an era. As the 1970s gave way to a new decade, the Steelers slid from their lofty perch and became just another NFL team, reaching the playoffs only four times during the 1980s.

The 1990s have been a different story. The turnaround began in 1992, the first season under Bill Cowher, when the Steelers went 11–5. By the middle of the decade, Cowher and a new crop of heroes had the Black and Gold back near the very top.

1995: Super Again

"Last year," former Steelers wide receiver Yancey Thigpen said in 1996, "we realized that when we put it all together, there wasn't a team in the National Football League that could beat us."[1] Thigpen was almost right.

The season started in anything but championship style. After beating Detroit in the opener, the Steelers lost four of their next six games. Then, however, they reeled off eight straight wins and eventually finished the regular season 11–5. After drubbing Buffalo and coming from behind to edge Indianapolis, they faced Dallas in Super Bowl XXX.

Pittsburgh fell behind early, 13–0, but fought back and pulled to within three points, 20–17, in the fourth quarter. Then the Steelers made a fatal mistake. Wide receiver Andre Hastings ran a pass route to the inside. Quarterback Neil O'Donnell threw the ball outside, right into the waiting hands of Dallas cornerback Larry Brown, and the Cowboys went on to win, 27–17.

"I was very proud of our football team," Cowher said after the game, "especially the way they responded after being down early. I think that was indicative of our 1995 season."[2]

The Price of Success

The Steelers continued to pile up winning seasons. It was hard to see how they did it, since so many players left the team to join other teams through free agency. From the end of the 1994 season until the beginning of the 1997 season, the Steelers lost twenty-two players.

After the 1995 Super Bowl season, quarterback Neil O'Donnell, linebacker Kevin Greene, running back Byron "Bam" Morris, and tackle Leon Searcy departed. People said the Steelers would be a much weaker team. Instead, they won their division again in 1996.

It was the same story after the 1996 season. All-Pro cornerback Rod Woodson, All-Pro linebacker Chad

The Pittsburgh Steelers Football Team

Jerome Bettis joined the Steelers for the 1996 season. Known as The Bus, it is not uncommon for Bettis to run over would-be tacklers.

Brown, and wide receivers Andre Hastings and Ernie Mills signed with other teams. "That's football," said Coach Bill Cowher. "We're not the only team that's losing players. We still have a strong nucleus. Guys who've been backups will have to step up."[3]

Filling the Holes

Carnell Lake, a big part of that nucleus, agreed with the coach. "Those losses are big losses, and when those guys left, they left big holes," he said. "It will definitely test our character, test us as a team to see if we can overcome these losses and repeat—and maybe win."[4]

1990s and Beyond

The Steelers did not simply sit still while other teams were signing its players as free agents. The Steelers signed a big one of their own, with All-Pro cornerback Donnell Woolford coming over from the Chicago Bears.

More players who figured to keep the Steelers on the winning track included Jerome Bettis, Greg Lloyd, All-Pro center Dermontti Dawson, Pro Bowl line-backer Levon Kirkland, wide receiver Charles Johnson, and Pro Bowl guard Will Wolford.

The Quarterback Question

One of the biggest questions facing the Steelers was at quarterback. Bill Cowher hoped he had found the right answer when he named Kordell Stewart as the starter before the 1997 season. Stewart, an outstanding quarterback at the University of Colorado, was considered by many to be too small to play that position in the NFL. In his first two seasons the Steelers decided to use him as a quarterback/receiver/running back. Because of this, he was nicknamed Slash.

"I'm capable of doing a lot of things," he said, "But I'm a quarterback. I've said that, and I will always say that. That Slash thing, that's fine and dandy. But I'm Kordell Stewart, and I'm a quarterback."[5]

The Winning Tradition

One thing the Steelers have going for them is tradition—not the losing tradition of the first forty years, but the winning tradition built over the last

The Pittsburgh Steelers Football Team

*S*tewart took over as the Steelers starting quarterback at the start of the 1997 season. Steelers fans hope Stewart will lead Pittsburgh back to the Super Bowl championship.

twenty-five years. Fans in Pittsburgh have become used to seeing some of the greatest players in the game, players like Terry Bradshaw, Franco Harris, Mel Blount, and Lynn Swann.

"While our goal is always to win a division championship, the difference is that it's now the standard," Cowher said. "We have put ourselves in the position where anything less than that may be perceived as a step back."[6]

Will the Steelers avoid a step back? Will they continue to win? "I don't see any reason why not," said Cowher. "It may not be easy, but life isn't easy."[7]

1990s and Beyond

STATISTICS

Team Record

The Steelers History

SEASONS	W	L	T	PCT.	PLAYOFFS	CHAMPIONSHIPS
1933–39	22	55	3	.294	—	None
1940–49	40	64	6	.391	0–1	None
1950–59	54	63	3	.463	—	None
1960–69	46	85	7	.359	—	None
1970–79	99	44	1	.691	14–4	Super Bowl IX, X, XIII, XIV
1980–89	77	75	0	.507	2–4	None
1990–97	80	48	0	.625	5–6	1995 AFC Championship

The Steelers Today

YEAR	W	L	PCT.	COACH	DIVISION FINISH
1990	9	7	.563	Chuck Noll	3
1991	7	9	.438	Chuck Noll	2
1992	11	5	.688	Bill Cowher	1
1993	9	7	.563	Bill Cowher	2
1994	12	4	.750	Bill Cowher	1
1995	11	5	.688	Bill Cowher	1
1996	10	6	.625	Bill Cowher	1
1997	11	5	.688	Bill Cowher	1

W=Wins (Regular Season)
L=Losses (Regular Season)
T=Ties (Regular Season)

PCT.=Winning Percentage
PLAYOFFS=Record in Playoffs
CHAMPIONSHIPS=Championships won

The Pittsburgh Steelers Football Team

Total History

W	L	T	PCT.	SUPER BOWL WINS
418	434	20	.491	4

Coaching Records

COACH	YEARS COACHED	RECORD	CHAMPIONSHIPS
Jap Douds	1933	3–6–2	None
Luby DiMello	1934	2–10	None
Joe Bach	1935–36, 1952–53	21–27	None
Johnny Blood	1937–39	6–19	None
Walt Kiesling	1939–40, 1941–44, 1954–56	30–55–5	None
Bert Bell	1941	0–2	None
Buff Donelli	1941	0–5	None
Jim Leonard	1945	2–8	None
Jock Sutherland	1946–47	13–9–1	None
John Michelosen	1948–61	20–26–2	None
Buddy Parker	1957–64	51–47–6	None
Mike Nixon	1965	2–12	None
Bill Austin	1966–68	11–28–3	None
Chuck Noll	1969–91	193–148–1	AFC Central Division, 1972, 1974–79, 1983–84 AFC 1974–75, 1978–79 Super Bowl IX, X, XIII, XIV
Bill Cowher	1992–	64–32	AFC Central Division, 1992, 1994–97 AFC 1995

Great Steelers' Career Statistics

PASSING

PLAYER	SEASONS	Y	G	ATT	COMP	YDS	TD
Terry Bradshaw	1970–83	14	168	3,901	2,025	27,989	212
Bobby Layne	1958–62	15	173	3,700	1,814	26,768	196
Neil O'Donnell	1991–95	7	87	2,519	1,429	16,810	79
Kordell Stewart	1995–	3	42	477	252	3,180	22

RUSHING

PLAYER	SEASONS	Y	G	ATT	YDS	AVG	TD
Jerome Bettis	1996–	5	78	1,491	6,187	4.1	31
Franco Harris	1972–83	13	173	2,949	12,120	4.1	91

RECEIVING

PLAYER	SEASONS	Y	G	REC	YDS	AVG	TD
Buddy Dial	1959–63	8	98	261	5,436	20.8	44
Louis Lipps	1984–91	9	110	359	6,019	16.8	39
John Stallworth	1974–87	14	165	537	8,723	16.2	63
Lynn Swan	1974–82	9	116	336	5,462	16.3	51

DEFENSE

PLAYER	SEASONS	Y	G	SACKS	INT	FUM
Mel Blount	1970–83	14	200	0*	57	13
Joe Greene	1969–81	13	181	66*	74	16
Jack Lambert	1974–84	11	146	8*	28	15
Greg Lloyd	1988–	10	131	53.5	10	15
Rod Woodson	1987–96	11	148	13.5	41	22

SEASONS=Seasons with Steelers   COMP=Completions   INT=Interceptions
Y=Years in NFL   YDS=Yards   FUM=Fumble Recoveries
G=Games   TD=Touchdowns
ATT=Attempts   AVG=Average

*Sacks were an unofficial statistic until the 1982 season.

The Pittsburgh Steelers Football Team

CHAPTER NOTES

Chapter 1: Immaculate Reception

1. Terry Bradshaw, *Looking Deep* (Chicago: Contemporary Books, 1989), p. 12.

2. Don Kowett, *Franco Harris* (New York: Coward, McCann & Geohegan, 1977), p. 9.

3. Ray Didinger, *Pittsburgh Steelers* (New York: Macmillan, 1974), p. 97.

4. Joe Tucker, *Steelers' Victory After Forty* (New York: Exposition Press, 1973), p. 233.

Chapter 2: The Long Climb

1. Ray Didinger, *Pittsburgh Steelers* (New York: Macmillan, 1974), p. 141.

2. Joe Tucker, *Steelers' Victory After Forty* (New York: Exposition Press, 1973), p. 40.

3. Abby Mendelson, *The Pittsburgh Steelers* (Dallas, Tex.: Taylor, 1996), p. 62.

Chapter 3: Men of Steel

1. Abby Mendelson, *The Pittsburgh Steelers* (Dallas, Tex.: Taylor, 1996), p. 45.

2. Ray Didinger, *Pittsburgh Steelers* (New York: Macmillan, 1974), p. 16.

3. Ibid., p. 13.

4. Larry Fox, *Mean Joe Greene and the Steelers' Front Four* (New York: Dodd, Mead, 1975), p. xiii.

5. Murray Chass, *Pittsburgh's Steelers: The Long Climb* (Englewood Cliffs, N.J.: Prentice-Hall, 1973), p. 108.

6. Terry Bradshaw, *Looking Deep* (Chicago: Contemporary Books, 1989), p. 116.

7. S. H. Burchard, *Sports Hero Franco Harris* (New York: Harcourt Brace Jovanovich, 1976), p. 49.

8. Don Kowett, *Franco Harris* (New York: Coward, McCann & Geohegan, 1977), p. 48.

9. Mendelson, p. 176.

10. Ed Bouchette, "Steelers Cupboard Is Not Bare Yet, Despite Talent Raids," *NFL Kickoff 97* (Los Angeles: National Football League Properties, Inc., 1997), p. 137.

Chapter 4: From Chief to Cowher

1. Lou Sahadi, *Steelers!* (New York: Times Books, 1979), p. 4.

2. Abby Mendelson, *The Pittsburgh Steelers* (Dallas, Tex.: Taylor, 1996), p. 15.

3. Ray Didinger, *Pittsburgh Steelers* (New York: Macmillan, 1974), p. 125.

4. Terry Bradshaw, *Looking Deep* (Chicago: Contemporary Books, 1989), p. 189.

5. Didinger, p. 12.

6. Joe Tucker, *Steelers' Victory After Forty* (New York: Exposition Press, 1973), p. 133.

7. Didinger, p. 29.

8. Pat Livingston, *The Pittsburgh Steelers* (Virginia Beach, Va.: Jordan, 1980), p. 105.

9. Murray Chass, *Pittsburgh's Steelers: The Long Climb* (Englewood Cliffs, N.J.: Prentice-Hall, 1973), p. 29.

10. Mendelson, p. 167.

11. Ibid., p. 185.

Chapter 5: Super Times Four

1. Lou Sahadi, *Steelers!* (New York: Times Books, 1979), foreword.

2. Pat Livingston, *The Pittsburgh Steelers* (Virginia Beach, Va.: Jordan, 1980), p. 106.

3. Abby Mendelson, *The Pittsburgh Steelers* (Dallas, Tex.: Taylor, 1996), p. 103.

4. Richard Rambeck, *Super Bowl X* (Mankato, Minn.: Creative Education, 1983), p. 29.

5. Richard Rambeck, *Super Bowl XIV* (Mankato, Minn.: Creative Education, 1983), p. 28.

6. Robert Oates, Jr., *Pittsburgh's Steelers* (Los Angeles: Rosebud Books, 1982), p. 74.

Chapter 6: 1990s and Beyond

1. Abby Mendelson, *The Pittsburgh Steelers* (Dallas, Tex.: Taylor, 1996), p. 173.

2. Ibid., p. 186.

3. "Pittsburgh Steelers," *Athlon Sports Pro Football* (Nashville: Athlon Sports Communications, 1997), p. 160.

4. Mendelson, p. 188.

5. Ibid., p. 185.

6. Ed Bouchette, "Steelers Cupboard Is Not Bare Yet, Despite Talent Raids," *NFL Kickoff 97* (Los Angeles: National Football League Properties, Inc., 1997), p. 136.

7. Ibid., p. 137.

GLOSSARY

cut—When a player is dropped from the team.

draft—The system by which college players are chosen by NFL teams. The teams choose in turn. The teams with the worst records choose first, and the better teams choose last.

fading back—The quarterback retreats, looking for a pass receiver, after taking the ball from the center.

free agency—The system that allows a player who has completed his contract with a team to sign with any other team.

instant replay—The system that gave an official seated in the press box the power, after viewing videotapes, to reverse decisions made by officials on the field. Instant replay is no longer in use.

pass rush—When defensive linemen charge forward trying to trap the quarterback behind the line of scrimmage.

playoffs—The system by which the teams with the best records each year meet in a series of games to determine a final champion.

Pro Bowl—A game played each year the week after the Super Bowl between teams of the best players from the National Football Conference and the American Football Conference.

sack—Tackling the quarterback behind the line of scrimmage. The NFL began keeping quarterback sacks as an official statistic in 1982.

scrambling—When the quarterback is forced to run away from pass rushers in order to avoid being sacked for a loss.

stiff-arm—When a player avoids a tackler by pushing him aside with the arm in which he is not carrying the football.

Super Bowl—The game between the NFC and AFC champions that is played each year to determine the NFL championship.

FURTHER READING

Bouchette, Ed. *The Pittsburgh Steelers.* New York: St. Martin's Press, Inc., 1994.

Goodman, Michael. *Pittsburgh Steelers*, 2nd edition. Mankato, Minn.: Creative Education, Inc., 1996.

Italia, Bob. *The Pittsburgh Steelers.* Minneapolis: Abdo & Daughters Publishing, 1996.

Lace, William W. *Top 10 Football Quarterbacks.* Springfield, N.J.: Enslow Publishers, Inc., 1994.

Majewski, Stephen. *Sports Great Jerome Bettis.* Springfield, N.J.: Enslow Publishers, Inc., 1997.

O'Brien, Jim. *Doing It Right: The Steelers of Three Rivers & Four Super Bowls Share Their Secrets for Success.* Pittsburgh: James P. O'Brien Publishing, 1985.

———. *Keep the Faith: The Steelers of Two Different Eras.* Pittsburgh: James P. O'Brien Publishing, 1997.

Prentzas, G. S. *Terry Bradshaw.* Broomall, Pa.: Chelsea House Publishers, 1994.

Savage, Jeff. *Top 10 Football Sackers.* Springfield, N.J.: Enslow Publishers, Inc., 1997.

Thornley, Stew, *Top 10 Football Receivers.* Springfield, N.J.: Enslow Publishers, Inc., 1995.

The Pittsburgh Steelers Football Team

INDEX

WHERE TO WRITE

Pittsburgh Steelers
300 Stadium Circle
Pittsburgh, PA 15212

WEBSITE

http://www.nfl.com/steelers

The Pittsburgh Steelers Football Team